Foxy

loses his tail

Colin and Jacqui Hawkins

Collins

An Imprint of HarperCollins*Publishers*

One morning Foxy woke up late. He jumped out of bed and got dressed very quickly.

"I'm late," said Foxy,
as he rushed to meet
his friends.

"Hello, Foxy," said Dog.
"Where's your tail?"

"Oh, no!" cried Foxy.

He had lost his tail.

They all looked for Foxy's tail.

Dog looked in the kitchen.

Badger looked in the bathroom. "It's not in here," he said.

Foxy looked in the toy cupboard, but only found his little sister.

Foxy and his friends looked everywhere, even under the bed. But all they found was an old sock.

Poor Foxy felt very sad.
"Cheer up, Foxy," said Badger.

"This sock will make a good tail," said Dog.

"Here's a pin," said Badger.
Dog tried to
pin the sock
onto Foxy's
dungarees.

"Ouch!" yelled Foxy.
Dog had stuck the pin
in Foxy's bottom.

"Sorry, Foxy," cried Dog.

"Look! What's this?"
said Badger.
"That's Foxy's tail,"
said Dog.
Silly Foxy. It was
tucked into his
dungarees all
the time.

Foxy felt very happy. Now they could all go out and play with Dog's kite.

"It's got a tail too," laughed Foxy.

Read more about Foxy and friends in
FOXY AND THE SPOTS

First published in Great Britain by HarperCollins Publishers Ltd in 1995 ISBN 0 00 198145 5 (hardback) 10 9 8 7 6 5 4 3 2 1
ISBN 0 00 664536 4 (paperback) 10 9 8 7 6 5 4 3 2 1 Text and illustrations copyright © Colin and Jacqui Hawkins 1995
The authors assert the moral right to be identified as the authors of this work. A CIP catalogue record for this title is available
from the British Library. All rights reserved. No part of the publication may be reproduced, stored in a retrieval system,
or transmitted in any form or by any means, electronic, mechanical, photocopying, recording or otherwise, without the
prior permission of HarperCollins Publishers Ltd, 77-85 Fulham Palace Road, Hammersmith, London W6 8JB
Printed and bound in Italy